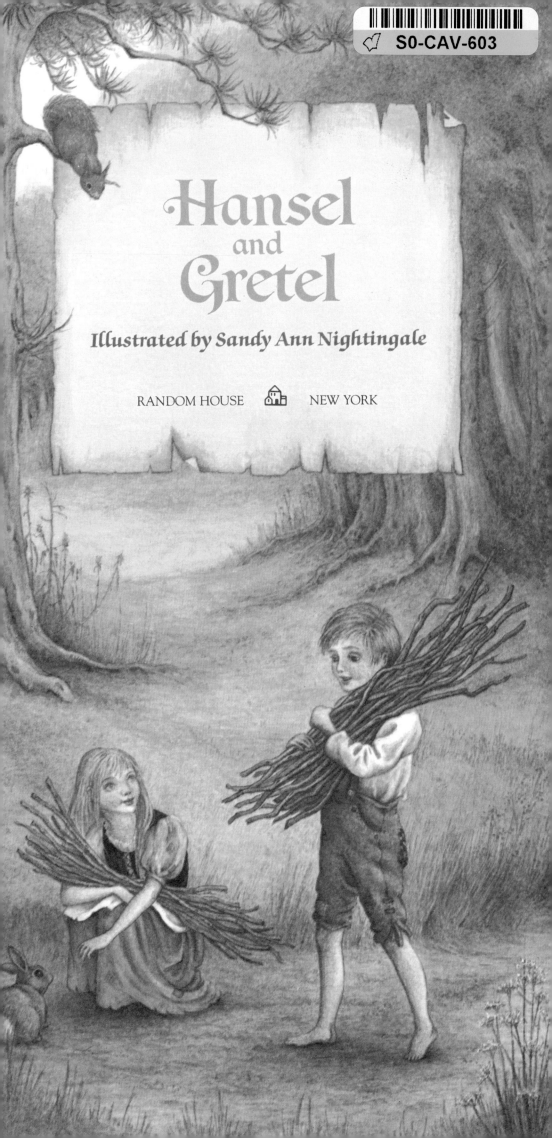

Hansel and Gretel

Illustrated by Sandy Ann Nightingale

RANDOM HOUSE   NEW YORK

Long, long ago at the edge of a great forest lived a poor woodcutter, his wife, and his two children. The boy was called Hansel and the girl was called Gretel. The woodcutter's wife was not the children's real mother. And she did not love them. Not even a little bit.

Times were hard. And there never was enough food on the table.

"Why should I have to share food with them?" the stepmother would shout at her husband. "I'm tired of being hungry all the time."

The woodcutter did not know what to say.

One night, when Hansel and Gretel were in bed, they heard their father and stepmother talking.

Hansel crept out of bed and stood by the door.

"What are they saying?" asked Gretel.

"Shhh," Hansel told her. "I'm trying to listen."

"We have only a little bread left," Hansel heard his stepmother say. "We have no choice but to get rid of the children. If we don't, we are all going to starve!"

"I do not want to hear this," said the woodcutter. He put his hands over his ears, but his wife made him listen anyway.

"Tomorrow morning we are going to take Hansel and Gretel deep into the forest and leave them there," she said. "Let them try and find their own food! Let them see what it is like to take care of themselves!"

"I can't do that!" cried the woodcutter. "They are my children."

"You must," his wife insisted. And she nagged at her husband until at last he agreed to her plan.

"Oh, Hansel!" whispered Gretel. "What is going to become of us?"

"Don't worry, Gretel," Hansel whispered back. "I have an idea."

Hansel climbed up on a chair and crawled out the window. He saw lots of shiny pebbles lying on the ground. They glittered like new coins in the moonlight. Hansel put a handful in a pouch and climbed back into their room.

Early the next morning the stepmother
shook Hansel and Gretel from their bed.

"Wake up! There is work to be done!"
she shouted. "We are all going to the forest
to chop wood. Here is your lunch." And
she handed each of them a small piece of
bread.

So the woodcutter and his family set off
into the woods, and as they walked, Hansel
dropped shiny pebbles onto the ground.

When they finally came to a clearing in
the woods, Hansel and Gretel's father made
a fire.

"Rest here, children," said the
stepmother. "We are going a little farther to
chop wood. We will be back soon."

By the time the sun had gone
down, the fire was almost out and
still no one had come to fetch Hansel
and Gretel. Gretel began to cry.

"Don't worry, little sister," said
Hansel. "Wait until the moon comes
up. Then we will find our way home.
You will see!"

And sure enough, when the moon
had risen, Hansel took Gretel by the
hand and they followed the path of
shiny pebbles all the way home. Their
father was overjoyed to see them, but
their stepmother was angry. Very,
very angry.

The next morning the stepmother told Hansel and Gretel they were going out into the forest again.

Hansel had no time to pick up any pebbles, so instead he dropped bits of bread to mark a path as they went into the forest. Hansel did not see that mice and birds were eating up all the bread he had dropped.

Once again the woodcutter and his wife left Hansel and Gretel all alone deep in the forest.

When night fell, Hansel took Gretel by the hand to lead her home. But the path was gone!

Hansel and Gretel were lost in the forest! All night long they wandered through the woods, but they could not find their way home.

Then, just as the sun came up, they saw a wonderful sight.

There before them was a little
house made of gingerbread and
candy. There were cookie tiles on
the roof, and the windows were
made of spun sugar.

Hansel and Gretel ran to the
house and began to eat it right
away.

All of a sudden a little old
woman poked her head out the
window.

"Nibble, nibble,
Like a mouse.
Who is nibbling
At my house?"

"Why, it's two little children!" the old woman said. "How lovely! Come in, come in! You both look very hungry and very tired."

"Oh, we are!" cried Hansel and Gretel. And without a second's thought they went inside the house.

The little old woman fed Hansel and Gretel cookies and cakes and then tucked them into a soft feather bed.

When they were asleep, the old woman cackled softly. "Now I've got you. And what a tasty meal you will make!" You see, she had only pretended to be kind. She was really a witch, and she liked nothing better than to eat up little children!

The next morning the witch put Gretel to work, cooking and cleaning the house. And she locked Hansel in a cage. She was going to eat him first, but she wanted to fatten him up a little.

The witch made sure that Hansel ate very well, and every day she would ask him to hold out his finger for her to pinch. She wanted to see how plump he had grown.

But Hansel was clever. He knew that witches cannot see well, so he would stick out a chicken bone for her to pinch.

"Why, you're still as thin as a stick!" the witch would cry.

At last the day came when the witch would wait no longer. "Fat or thin, I am going to eat you now!" she told Hansel. She ordered Gretel to light the oven.

After the oven was lit, the witch said, "Crawl in, girl, and see if the fire is hot enough."

"But I don't know how," said Gretel. "You must show me."

"Stupid girl!" shouted the witch. "See how easy it is." And the witch stuck her head in the oven.

That was the moment Gretel was waiting for! With all her might, she shoved the witch into the oven and slammed the door.

"The witch is dead!" Gretel shouted to her brother, and she let him out of his cage. They hugged each other. "We are free! We are free!"

Hansel and Gretel loaded their pockets with jewels they found in a wooden chest, and then they ran out of the house as fast as they could.

By the next morning Hansel and Gretel had found their way home. How happy their father was to see them! Their stepmother had gone away for good, and with the jewels from the witch's house, their troubles were over. Hansel and Gretel and their father lived happily ever after.